For Tid and Suzy

two lions

Text and illustrations copyright © 2020 by Ged Adamson

Published by Two Lions, New York
www.apub.com

Amazon, the Amazon logo, and Two Lions are trademarks of Amazon.com, Inc., or its affiliates.

ISBN-13: 9781542092715
ISBN-10: 154209271X

The illustrations were created using watercolor and pencil.
Book design by Tanya Ross-Hughes

Printed in China
First Edition
10 9 8 7 6 5 4 3 2 1

BIRD HUGS

Ged Adamson

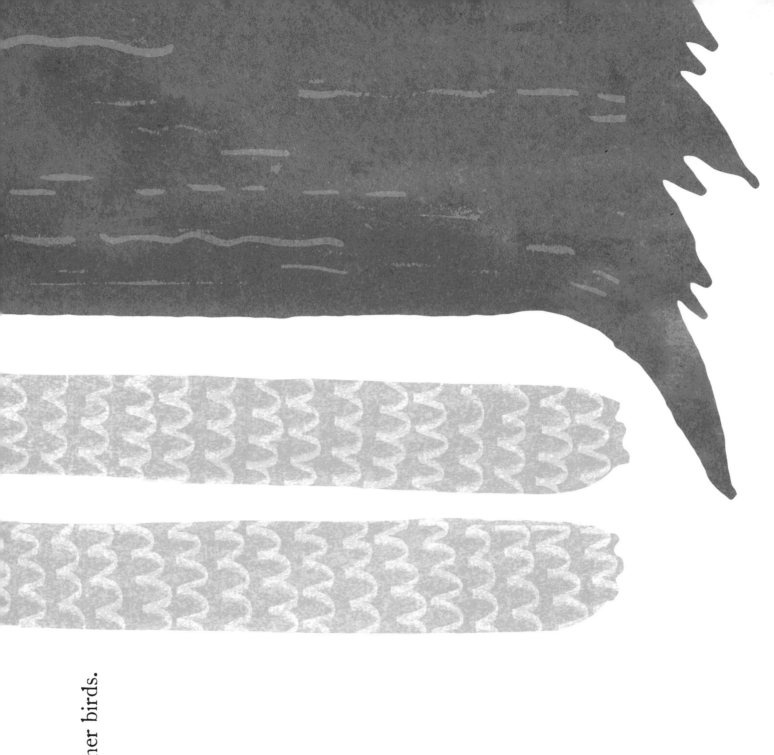

Bernard wasn't like other birds.

When he was a baby,
he didn't know he was different.

Life was simple. And fun!

Then Bernard's friends began to fly.

No matter how many times he tried,
it was something he couldn't seem to do himself.

One by one, the other birds left
in search of new places.
"I'll learn to fly soon, won't I?"
said Bernard.
"Of course you will," said Orla.

But the next day, she was gone too.
Bernard was all alone.

Maybe he just needed a little help?

"That's right, Lawrence," said Bernard.
"Keep pecking that rope."

...groan...

But he wasn't.

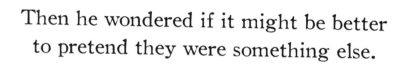

Embarrassed by his useless wings,
he tried to make them smaller.

Then he wondered if it might be better
to pretend they were something else.

A scarf, for instance?

A nice big bow?

It was hopeless. Bernard felt utterly sorry for himself.
He found a lonely branch and made it his home.

Days turned into nights. Seasons changed.

Different creatures came and went.
Bernard barely noticed them.

But then, one evening, he heard a sound.

It was coming from someone even
more dejected than Bernard.

"I feel very sad and I'm not sure why!"
wailed the orangutan.

Bernard jumped up and, with his long wings, gave the orangutan a BIG HUG.

The orangutan stopped crying and sighed.
After a while, he stood up and stretched.

"That's made me feel a whole lot better," he said.
"Thank you, kind bird."

Back at his branch,
Bernard thought that maybe
his wings were good for
something after all.

For the first time
in a long while,
he slept soundly
and woke refreshed.

Which was just
as well . . .

HUGS!

Bernard hugged a bear

and a rabbit

and a whole group of birds.

hee!
hee!

He hugged a very
ticklish crocodile

SLIP!

and a very slippery frog.

hug?

Even a worm wanted a hug
(which, you'll agree, was pretty
brave of the worm).

Now every morning, without fail,
there was a line.

The animals told Bernard their problems.

It can be lonely at the top of the food chain.

And he listened.

Bernard didn't feel sorry for himself anymore.
And all the hugging had made his wings feel strong.

Maybe even strong enough for . . .

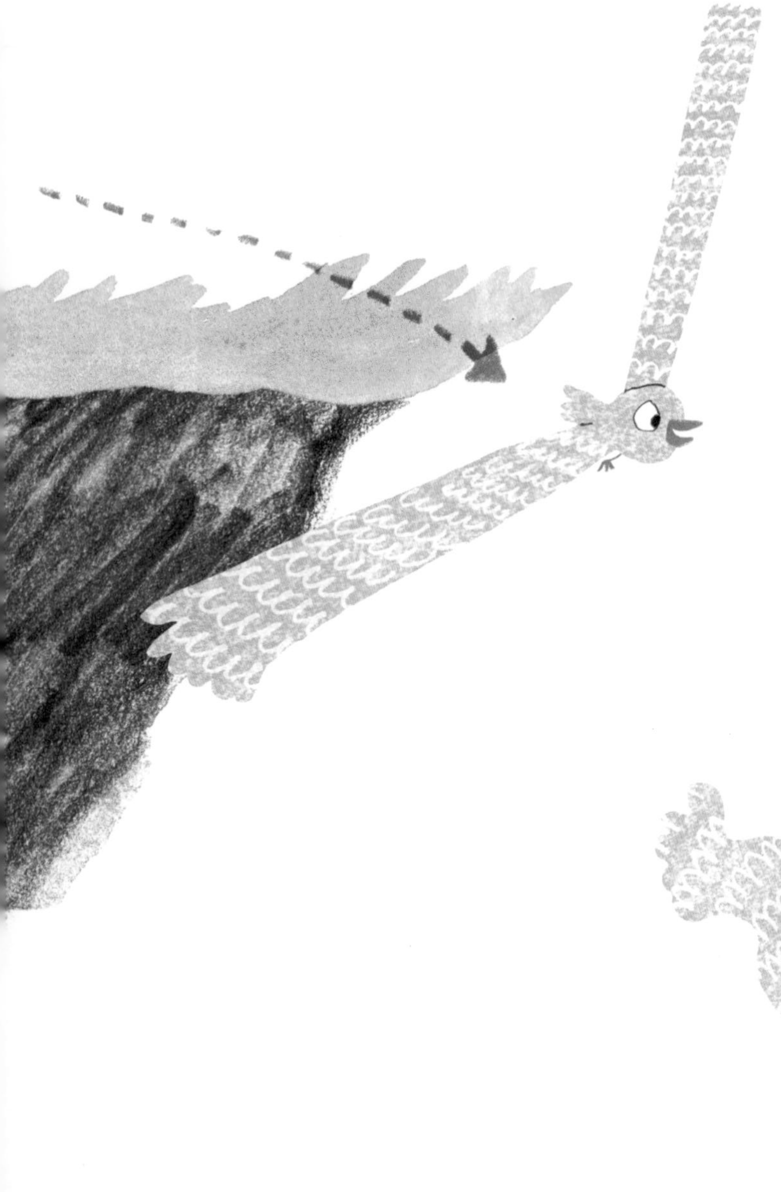

. . . flying!

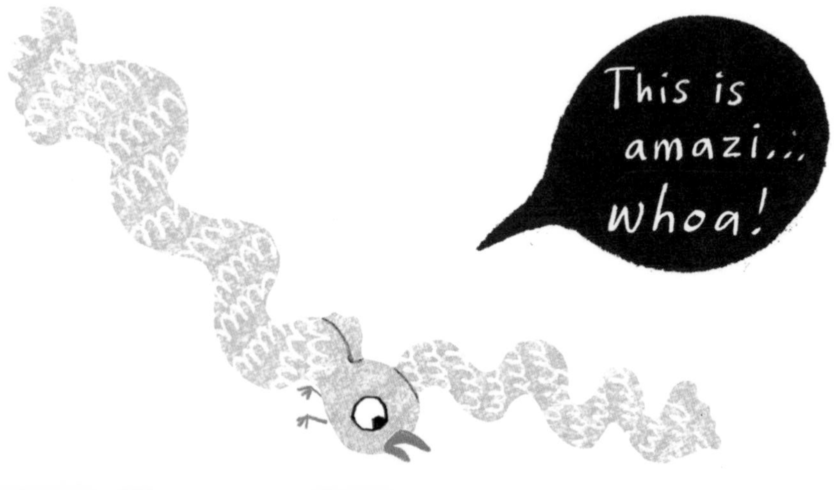

CRASH!

"There's more to life than flying,
I suppose," said Bernard.

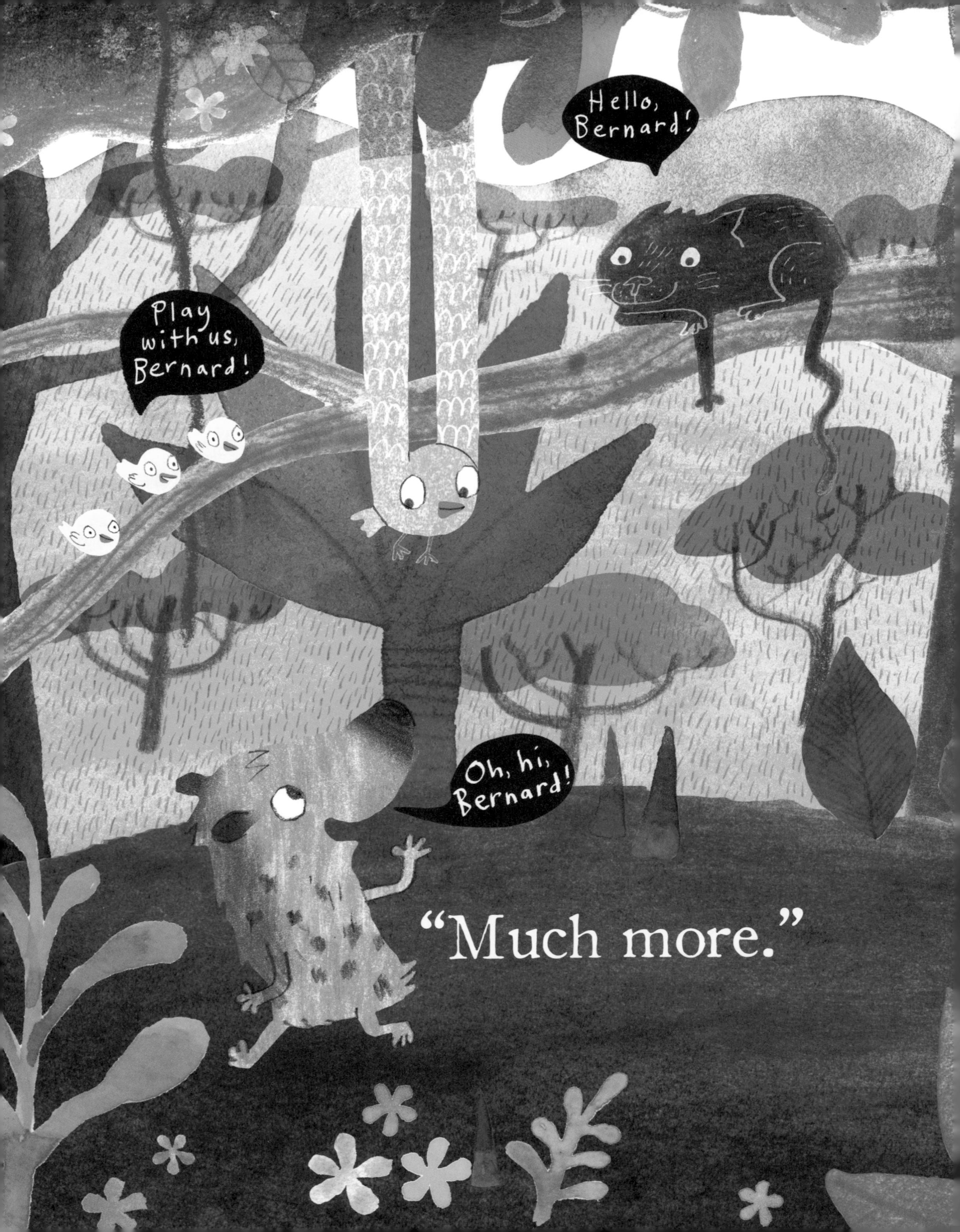

"Much more."

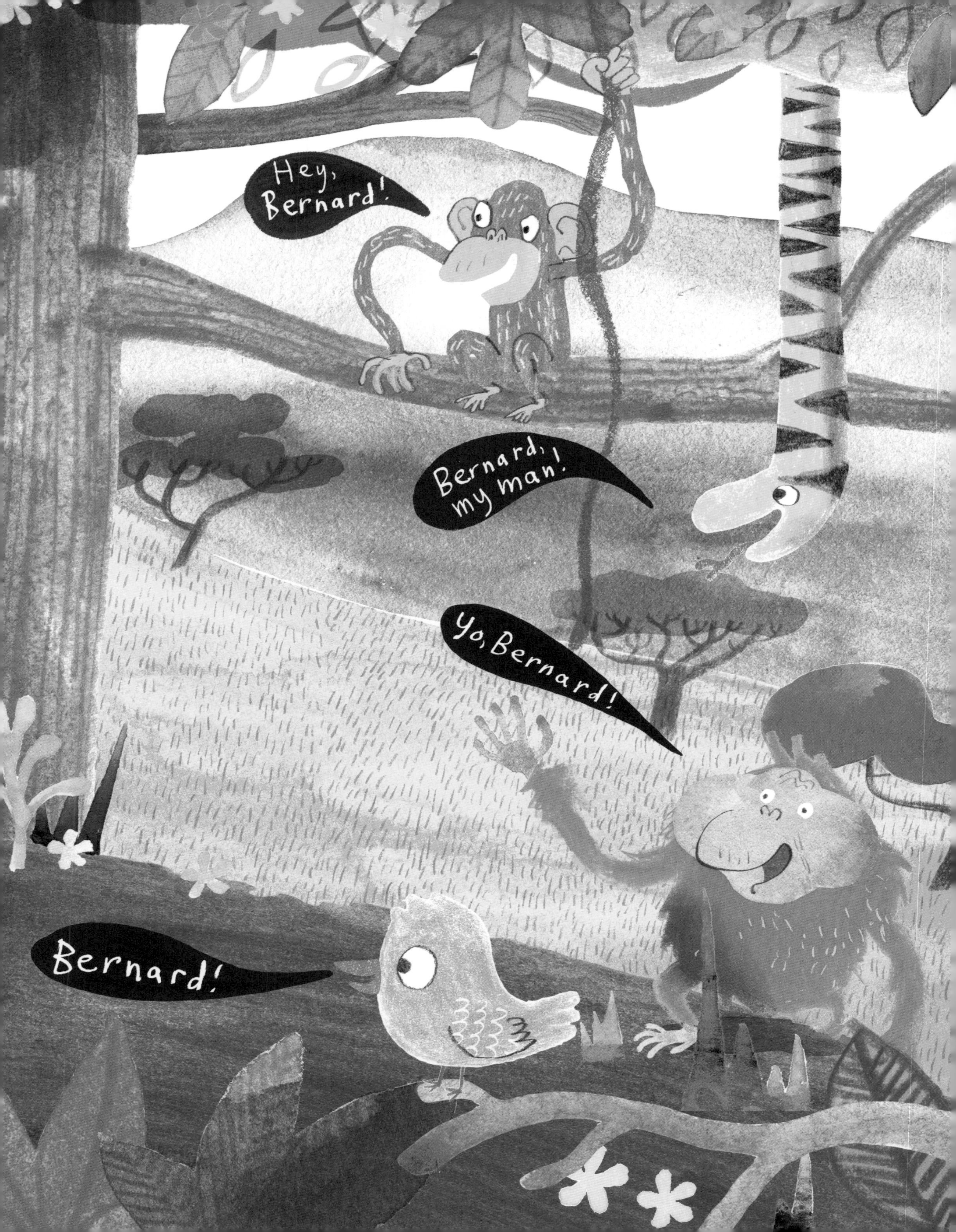
Hey, Bernard!
Bernard, my man!
Yo, Bernard!
Bernard!

Bernard discovered that helping the other animals
had given him something he hadn't expected:
new friends!

And friends can help you do anything!

Wheeeee!